The Transparence Of November / Snow

Quarry Press

The Transparence Of November / Snow

Roo Borson & Kim Maltman

Some of these poems have appeared previously in *Arc, The Canadian Forum, Canadian Literature, Dandelion, event, The Fiddlehead, Grain, The Literary Half-Yearly (India), Nebula, New Quarterly, Origins, Poetry Canada Review, Poetry Toronto, This Magazine, Toronto Life, Waves, Wot.*

The publisher thanks the Canada Council for financial assistance in producing this book.

Copyedited by Allan Brown and Christine Niero. Cover designed by Allison Warne.

Canadian Cataloguing in Publication Data

Borson, Roo, 1952-
    The Transparence of November; Snow

Poems.
ISBN 0-919627-30-7

1. Canadian poetry (English) — 20th century.
I. Maltman, Kim, 1950- II. Title. III. Title: Snow.

PS8553.0736T73 1985   C811'.54'08   C85-090160-X
PR9199.3.B67T73 1985

Typeset by Sykes & Sykes Business Communications, Gananoque, Ontario.
Printed by Hewson & White Ltd., Kingston, Ontario.

Quarry Press
P.O. Box 1061
Kingston, Ontario
K7L 4Y5

CONTENTS

THE TRANSPARENCE OF NOVEMBER

TRUST

WARMTH

GRID

TYRANNY

SNOW

for V.T.

THE TRANSPARENCE OF NOVEMBER

THE TRANSPARENCE OF NOVEMBER

The orchestra of the dark tangled field.
The moon holds the first note.

Silver-grey, the old barn leans a little,
just beginning to rise.

Since early autumn the poplars
have been racing one another
and are almost here.

Whatever small flowers
I may have mentioned in summer:
forget them.

DOVE

The bird will smother under its own wing tonight.
Still the night will get colder.
The bird is in the thornapple tree, I can see
where the branches prick at the moon.
This bird is the shape of a dove. What do I know?
The clouds are lit up like the spotlit pictures of Christ
in out-of-the-way churches, churches with dirt on the floor.
The clouds are full of shadows, and staves.
The dove flew too near them, and is pierced
by its own quills. See how he quivers
with what the coldest night of the year
has in mind for him. When I touch his back
with my little finger, nothing but a quick shiver
that melts away. He is lost,
he has forgotten
that he ever existed.

PEARLS

The swan glides comfortably on the pond.
Soon the pond will be ice, but the swan
doesn't know this yet. Its feathers iridesce,
pearls of water clinging to its sides.
The swan has almost fallen into its dream
of a lake without bottom,
meanwhile drifting on silver-plated water,
the water of night, of the earth,
a pond like a small hand mirror.
A young girl, shaken too early
by one of the ways of growing up
has come here to stand
with her arms crossed over her breasts, chilly,
wishing she were anything other than human.
When she looks up you can see
a few tears left over,
the moon gliding across them.
The huge pearl of the moon.

CYGNUS

On the pond at night a solitary swan drifts. Softly
she dips her head to feed, the surface ripples,

the moon is a long molten tongue.
Nothing speaks. The young birds have left.

Has the wind taken them? Overhead
the great swan floats as if at anchor. It is August, nearly

winter, an end of things. And the small wind that stirs
        in the trees chatters sadly saying
swan, swan where are your young.

UPSET, UNABLE TO SLEEP, I GO FOR A WALK
AND STUMBLE UPON SOME GEESE

Bright dime
cut in two, one half
in the sky, the other fallen on the pond,
but no one will bother to pick it up,
the moon will never be whole again.
Up and down the grassy hillocks
they follow one another, walking
in groups under the grey glow of the moon.
I haven't even startled them, this is no hour
for a human. Together here they act
differently, like themselves,
warm-blooded, clumsy, bitching
at one another in a common language.
I wish I were asleep. They are large and warm.
I'd like to hold one of them,
hold, be held.

WINTER

Along the blue edge of trees

high winter stars
like clappers without bells.

Then a voice: wood being chopped.
The words pronounced in a strange, careful accent.

DANGER

The badger digs its burrow. Deep.
(No matter how you dig you will not unearth it.)

The horses are half-wild. See how the mustang
turns into the wind, see how he tosses his head.

Nearby a man builds a house and steps inside.
On one of the low hills a coyote bays.

It is young.
It has left the litter.

TRUST

PASTORALE

With a lurch, as if from long disuse,
the huge machinery of night starts up again.
Out of the ground, between the thick black rows of
shadow soil, the shadow plants crawl,
and beneath their shade the shadow animals,
the shadow siege of ruts and holes
overflowing, swarming through the fields
like great soft beetles.
What could move the branches of that willow so?
The wind,
only the wind.
A lantern on a fencepost,
falling.
Shadows.
Now the owl is awake,
the grass a labyrinth of small sounds.
The shadow moon is high.
The owl flaps once and vanishes,
its feathers soft and soundless.
(Far off: farm lights.)
Small shivering sounds.
The blood-colored wind that ripples through the shadow rye.

BARN

Half twisted, the abandoned barn
leans toward the grass at night,
split at the seams to let the stars in,
an observatory for the dead animals,
their bones scattered in the grass,
to look at what they have lost
or never had.
And the moon frosted like the lace doily
on which an unlit kerosene lamp sits
in the farmhouse whose door has been missing
how long? — we are each alone here,
walking on two legs. Underfoot, twigs crackle,
like a fire lit by unhuman hands.

DEPENDENCE IN WINTER

Snowshoes on the shed wall
aching for the open fields, the leather laces
dreaming themselves into the skin of the first horse.
The rays of the whole woodpile are cradled
by the lantern's stored memory
of fall, the painstaking days.
Getting to know the spider that slides off
and scampers into crevices, each piece
as I pull it from the pile
beautifully twisted, preserved.
Welcoming that spider.
Snowshoes on the shed wall.
Open fields.

FOX

All day the fox rests in its burrow, wary.
Then it's dusk. The hills go dark, even with their coat of grain,

and the sky is red, red and cautious like the fox,
it won't come out into the full daylight,
it carries the night caught in the fur of its back.

Fox, says the moon, where are you,
where are you hiding in your dark coat?
(The fox puts on its shadow.)

Fox, says the owl, are you stealing my food,
where are you?
(The fox puts on its shadow.)

(And the farmer is asleep in his house.
Too dark to hunt foxes,
even the moon is no help.)

Fox, says the fieldmouse, where are you?
Find another kill tonight.
(The fox puts on its shadow.)

Only the air hears, the air is too calm,
it hears the fox coming and makes way.
(The fox puts on its shadow.)

FIELD MOUSE

The late afternoon woods are tall and deep,
full of browns quivering with sun going down.
The owl puts none of this into language,
only into dreams neglected now by his body
which flaps away from the tree where he was resting.
He watches the sweet
pocket of fur full of blood which he is about to puncture.

The moon guides him to it like a hand.

WOOD

Most of a life is roots and bark,
the dead cells, packed together,
channels for the day to flow through
up toward the head. The head
which by now has grown
far from the ground and rustles with secrets,
the hush of green, the sudden fruit.
What do you say to this now?
Head,
high up,
you who cast your shadow over everything?

RABBIT

The rabbit huddles in the grass.
Its eyes are cold, so it blinks.
The grass is tall and green
as if it could do anything
but the clouds merely charge overhead
in a replay of great battles.
The chicken fence lets all the wind in
and a speck of sun glints from one of the wires.
The rabbit doesn't know what it is to be owned.
Its pink eyes close against the cold
and its ears fold back.
It knows the smell of a garden,
the sound of approaching feet.
The feel of keeping its eyes closed anyway,
for away deep inside it is warm
where the blood tangles,
in the cold brilliant grass.

TRUST

Between the faded trees of evening
a troop of cattle hobbles down.
One behind another,
they move like covered wagons,
loose wheels over stones.
Under the few iceblue stars
they have come down from the high fields
and stand with their faces in the pond,
spokes of a broken wheel.
All at once
the whole group turns to move off,
following the starlight as it strikes
their broad faces,
leaving the ripples of tongues
to settle on the pond.
And that silent look comes over it,
the stars reappearing
where no one can touch them.

WARMTH

CIRCA 1930, COOL DAWNS

After the long day's labor, home.
The roar and chug of machinery since dawn
now calm, the light mist clear above the night-chilled fields,
hot noon sun, the smell of dust at midday,
fine drifting dust that coats the windward side
of fences, burns the mouth and eyes.
The sting of sweat all afternoon, a few hawks
lazy overhead, wings spread to catch the thermals.
Sound of thunder far off and no rain.
Days of straw, slow wheeling heat,
the work too easily made futile.
Debt that comes full circle in a year.
Sometimes too the smell of skin,
worn raw or sour with defeat,
that rises on the long road home.

STORMLIGHT

The pond glossed
whose depths remain
untouched.

Silent, sideways, white
the eggs
among the loosened chickens.

The air inside the barn
snorts and stamps once
without the barn moving.

Deep inside
the mare tosses, flinches,
the gleaming nap of hair
flown up between the eyes.
Stormlight along the muzzle.

Somewhere in the sky
big guns are beginning.
On the kitchen table
the loaves grow stony, grudging
the anniversary of wheat.

Under the table
the dog Shep,
flattened to a puddle,
quivering with stormbreeze,
learning to wait.

Shep. Who is alone,
who has learned his own name.

WARMTH

Seen from outside, through the frost,
the single light above the table flares and gutters.
Steam drifts from the soup pot,
vertical against the house's heat.
To the small boy upstairs sleeping
there is nothing but that warmth,
the rush of breathing, of blood inside the ear.
Not yet dawn and outside there are already
chores to be finished,
a lumbering father's body,
like a tree, clouded in breath,
that pushes through the snow in front of it.
When the footsteps come to the chickenyard
it means food. To the rabbit hutch,
food also. Then the wind shifts
and the small animals ruffle and close their eyes,
and the footsteps are gone, and that light,
and there is only the wind. The wind,
which does not kill because it needs nothing of this world.

SWEET BASIL

Until at last there is no light to see by,
only a cold wick of moon,
and the lantern of night has no edges.
Then the feet tramping up dust along the road,
past acres of tomatoes black as lumps of coal,
home to the lamp and a thick white plate
flecked with red and black,
basil, tomato, the tears
of the onion,
and a glass, a glass
brimmed with wine, the wine a man has made himself,
thick and purple as the blood returning to the heart.
And so for a man who thinks himself to be
only as good as what he has made,
this wine is a measure, this meal
an accounting of all his days, their worth and flavor.
Alcohol shimmers down the empty glass.
Heat over the empty hills. At noon
a man moves like a minute hand,
in slow jerks, and now
his hands are nearly useless.
How simple, how twisted,
that a man can grow to hate
the yield of all his labor,
the blameless ripeness of the vine.
Smoky incense of basil through the window.
Shadowed, wrinkled hills.
Basil which comes back every year
unchanged. Then bed.
Through the window,
but from the wrong side of it,
the boy who went missing
this afternoon from another village peers in
on that disorder, the unearthly white
of that body floating in the blankets, like his father's.

Then the wind flicks at a branch in the great tree overhead
and he turns, turns
in that willowy boy's body,
barely a sound as he slips through the fields.

THE TRELLIS

The old man listens to the rustle of the grape leaves
on the trellis by the window where the moon lies tangled,
cold and sickly, covered with dew.
A night like the eye of a storm,
a night that swallows everything
and leaves the stomach empty.
All day he has worked in a black anger, pruning and tying,
coaxing the vines to bear above the yard,
and now it is night again and the house restless,
restless as the knobbed hands of a carpenter that lie
useless in his lap, longing for something to tear.
Only the thunder in the distance,
like an empty stomach. Lightning
that spreads its eerie glow between the leaves.
What he remembers now is how he feared his father,
all the words that will not be digested.
For now his own sons are grown and useless,
and his only daughter, whom he never
laid a hand on, lately has become
sly and fickle, and the moon waits at the window of her room,
waits, blighting the grapes, saying yes, yes.

CLARY

Already night has settled on the pond.
This is years ago now,
and it is the last time the footsteps will
pass like this, amid the murmur of frogs,
the fine chill of the crickets.
Summer scatters a hundred living stars on the water
and the warm road rises, stilled with perfume.
Then we are gone.
Clary, I remember how we stood there,
almost touching. One by one
the cattle drifted back,
the fences once again were
insurmountable.
That charged erotic lassitude that overtook us,
how strongly it comes back.
All night I've stood and let it wash against
skin that has changed itself
a hundred times over,
the closed-in road, Clary,
the wild almond smell of that old
unhindered melancholy.

NIGHT TRAIN

And so the dark country is passing by,
the slow rain of beautiful white lights
in the cadence of towns.
A church that turns
its back on us in passing.
Lit main streets that itch. Tonight
no conceits, just the rails
like a heart coming up from below
to silence my own.

Porch lights that call and call.

GRID

GRID

One after another the lights of the houses
wink off, leaving, more and more, the night,
the cool dim grass that reaches up toward it,
soft and moist. A few streetlamps still burn
on the main roads and the sidewalks of certain
residential districts will be kept safe all night
by the light of others, but most of the city is in
darkness. Over the power grid a quiet descends.
Lights of rooming houses go out
and power is fed back to the grid. Office towers
brighten momentarily but this too goes unnoticed.
In one of the houses someone is still awake, reading.
Through the shade of the lamp the yellow light
spills out and prowls the room. All that remains of the city
are the shadows on the wall, shadows
and the almost audible hum of the power lines.
Soon the page ends and sleep comes.
The lamp goes dark. By morning that surge of power
will have been transformed, diluted through the
labyrinth of wires. On the grid
now the last house slumbers, immense and empty,
threaded with power. All night the dynamos churn.
All night people's lives are being joined to other people's lives.

JULY

Blue sky that holds off at a distance,
you can follow the pine trunks all the way up with your eye
to the high branches stilled in sunlight
where birds come and go
from here to the next county.
You can sit forever in an evening
spitting melon seeds,
twisting around the tongue
the few fibers that held
a whole mouthful of sweet water.
It is possible to swallow this
and all of childhood in one gulp,
along with all the wrongs that have not yet happened,
blessing them in advance.
Bright melon sliced open on the table
with all of summer leaking out of it.
Still the children call to one another in the streets
not wanting to come in, but on a night like this
if they stayed out they would learn how to float
like the moon through the pine branches.
On the table the half-eaten melon
is a cave of red meat and black stars,
pale rinds float in the grass,
and the big neighborhood dog comes to stand
like a hand stuffed into too small a glove.

HISTORY

The black dog trotting into the wind
gaily, as if every day were his birthday.
Under his lips he wears the smile of a skeleton.
The bushes whimper a little, like grown dogs,
while the wind pulls off their leaves
and the trees creak
as if a door might suddenly
fly open to another world.
Outside the corner grocery hothouse flowers
lean in buckets of water.
Very soon the women's painted lips and
painted toenails will glow dully underground.
Very soon the men's grey hats will perch
like stuffed doves on the closet shelves.

BARGE

Along the street the crowds
pole their way, laden with cargo: thoughts
that drift and drift and
come to nothing. Evening.
Bodies stiff from labor.
Solitary faces that will
disappear without a ripple.
Commerce puts down anchor for the night.
The dark prow of humanity pushes on.

JUST BEFORE DAWN

At the hour just before dawn
the streetlamps enter their deep irony.

The air is damp with the submerged wildness
of October, the wind that would shatter
all the trees at once if no one were looking.

At the hour when the rodents have barely managed
to conceal themselves, the streets are dark and empty
as if no one were alive.

The wind crescendos in the trees again and again
in huge waves that would knock you over
if they were made of anything but air.

The wind makes the fallen leaves scramble.
The ground tries to pull everything into it,
calling without a sound.

A book fallen in the grass:
who knows how long it's lain there full of shadows,
shadows of men who did things, civilizations.
Wet with uncut crystals of dew.

The bright red mailbox on the corner
full of letters lying in the dark,
from the world to the world.

SOUNDLESS

It is the season of apples. People
are carrying them on little trays,
beside the heaped plates, through the cafeteria.
They sit down and, deliberately, eat.
Outside the wind runs around
with an aimlessness akin to human thought.
We sit here tasting. Is that all?
The flavors are good. The wind has turned
our cheeks the color of apples.
At night the headlights are driven
like pitchforks into the huge glass buildings.

OWNERSHIP

Office buildings, deep into the night.
The smoke of factories reflected on the rails.
And at the gate, a guard who sits and smokes
while the ships are loaded.
Another thousand metric tonnes of grain.
All night the smoke drifts up.
Then it is dawn,
a factory whistle sounds,
more grain moves out across the rails.
The black figure, for example,
of a head against the glass twilight.

TYRANNY

SNOW

Still a way to go till home.
Don't panic little one,

run away and play, it's only your brain turning over in its sleep.
See how the dark and light happen at once.

Thick flakes of snow drifting through the headlights:
a thousand windows cut loose from their moorings.

Walk here; slowly store lights pass, it is nearly Christmas.
Who lives here? What to do? Recognize the many shapes of one thing.

Into a path a cat pounces, snow hanging from its mouth,
the feathers of some bird too diffuse for us to comprehend.

GREY

Six doors.
Along the street, on one side,
each the same,
a wreath for Christmas hung on each door,
at the center,
like the frames of one-way mirrors
but from which who looks?
from what and into what?
except for one —
one door —
a door like the others,
only at the lower corner, a small
thin cat which is grey, grey
as snow is, falling through the still
smudged air, grey as the ash
that spills from overturned
garbage cans in alleys behind
bars and restaurants at night, grey
as the cold that settles in at nightfall.
It is a small thing, this incident
among all incidents, this small grey cat
that failed to learn in time,
to turn wild,
too tame to know anything but waiting,
waiting at one door among many doors,
a door which is familiar,
which does not open and will not,
the world inside it having changed,
given way to another in which there is no room
for cats — a small thing
of which there will be
perhaps no more than this momentary sadness, or
inability, the ease with which
pain is administered
without meaning or intention.

And so it passes,
one of many things that in the end
have little consequence, undeniable but distant,
a small detail that singles out this
one door among many, at this instant,
and only for this instant,
without sound, or sense or color,
except the soft grey color
which touches the fur, the frostbitten ears,
the quiet wait into night as the wind comes.

THE GARDENER WHO WAS TAKEN FROM HIS HOME DURING THE WAR AND DID NOT TRUST THOSE WHO WOULD NOT LOVE FLOWERS

Out of the silent tangle of frost and dirt,
so strong now nothing dares to stop it,
the first pale blossoms, coaxed out early for a day like this
by Howard Nishomoto (since deceased)
are rising,
frail perfume adrift
along the path
of flat pink stones, the bridge across
the garden's little creek, the railing that is cool
to the touch and holds
the bride — all forms of happiness.
How sad it is on this,
the last day of heaven, of grace,
the end of certainty,
the end, in fact, of Howard Nishomoto,
that everywhere this soft new green
should stumble into being.
A day like this — the last —
and anyone would want to find out why
but there are no reasons
and all injustices are one injustice.
And then it all goes away,
into the pocket of history,
and someone says, someone with hurt sunken gums
they are ashamed of, someone who always
smiles with lowered face,
if this is the truth,
if we are to be shown today,
please, can't someone get me my teeth.

ALTRUISM

Even at noon the sun is weak. It flies too high.
It falls to the ground, exhausted,
a lone sparrow, hungry, nothing left to feed it.
A hundred people pass, a thousand. Only after some time
one among them stops and picks it up.
The ground is frozen, dry.
He cups it in his hands. Its breathing fills his arms.
A bit of stale bread from his pocket, that's all, useless,
a million of them would fit onto the head of a pin.
By now his hands are warm.
He puts the sparrow down.
What will you eat now sparrow? What will you eat?
So cold, so cold, no end in sight.

COAL

Above the roofs the first light,
bleached of depth, in all directions,
snow above the houses,
black with coal, the muffled glow
of lives asleep inside,
half-gone or
wished away by pieces.

It is next to nothing,
the cough of a child,
the endless snow of coal —
a candle for such a life.

Yet from this moment on we are
caught, lost on that street.

THE GATHERERS OF DEAD WOOD

— after the painting by van Gogh

When the fire burns low we leave.
Against the cold our clothes are
little more than rags. Early outside, barely light,

the snow drifts and drifts.
We gather dead wood. A hand held
close to fire is red, the sun above the low hills.

So that we shall not fear death
the priests have blessed us, saying
that the meek shall inherit the earth.

I see the warmth of their houses, smell
the perfume on their breath.
Anger they say drags the soul

down toward damnation.
Our clothes are little more than rags.
When the fire burns low we leave.

TYRANNY

All day they march past with their fine boots
and their bodyguards and shield their eyes.
The glare of the sun is great, the buildings white.
They do not see us.

Even the young girls sent to them at night
they crush beneath them, clucking and cooing,
caressing the soft shivering bellies.

So many dead. They shield their eyes.
Death is coming toward us along all the roads.
In the heat and the flies.

This morning from the street the sound of gunfire
and the long silence.
In the street at noon the soldier still dying.

Now it is dark. Pray for the soldier's soul,
take the boots from his feet. Who will
plant the fields? Feed our wives and children? I ask this

humbly for I am afraid. Tonight we go forever across the fields,
toward the smoke of the new moon, the rebel fires.
Death will come to them from the mountains.

SNOW

COMFORT

The old church slips toward senescence.
Bit by bit the stone walls split and settle,
letting in small animals they held at bay
a century or more. The old church
has fallen on hard times, the roof gone,
most of the steeple toppled.
Once it dominated an entire countryside,
that steeple, every waking hour,
harvest, danger, kinship, the quiver
of generations. Such a long time now
that even Christ might pass and not see,
not remember those who left with nothing but the
few belongings on their backs.
There was a time when the church
protected them, shedding a glow of
comfort and prosperity,
but now only the small animals
are free. They inhabit the church
as they were meant to, without fear.
And then the birds return to the alcoves,
and where the saints once stood, they perch,
and forgive them,
and set them free.

WILD HORSES

There are horses of sorrow that
never change their expressions,
their faces hang like shadows, as if
suspended from something bright,
bright horses whose shadows
these faces are, horses
that roamed like an ocean wave across the plains
and left them bare, and the sky tells nothing
of where they went, the sky is too bare.

The horses (the dark ones) stand now in a stable,
no one comes to release them,
each face framed in its stall
of beaten wood, wood marred by weather
and the flanks of these horses
that have been here too long, restless,
with nowhere to go.

Now and then riders come to ride them
over the plains, but their expressions do not change,
fixed in the fixed wind, though they are roving
over territory those others owned
when they lived here, they are saddled with riders
and their shadows, they are shadows.

THE HEART FALLS ASLEEP

The heart falls asleep,
not gradually, not knowing how exactly, but all at once,
like a suddenly-emptied thing, a cloth doll
tossed into a corner and left there,
accidental, helpless, a light being shut off, the
hum of trains, a man in the subway
pushing the mop in front of him for the last time
tonight, the spirit gone out of it,
the last feeling, a candle about to go out
in a pool of its own wax
that melts through at the last minute.
The heart falls asleep,
the quiet sleep of machines, of finding pitch,
of running smoothly, the sleep of economy, of
no hesitation to the sound,
not of fatigue, or forgetfulness,
or envy, just straight ahead.
The heart falls asleep.
Why not? What has to be done it does
with its eyes closed. Why bother,
the ribs hum, the body hums,
things will not hang together, even the hand turns away
unfinished, nothing comes out right
and so the heart falls asleep,
because there is too much it wants,
so much that even in its sleep it can't stay still,
it stretches, it makes a small sound, a sound
like metal fatiguing, a line being scratched on glass,
things of no order, no focus,
and then it says without knowing it
that it does not want you to be gone.

WILD STRAWBERRIES

And so I've reduced it all
to a sadness at the back of the throat.
No touch so explicit, no word.
The black and white forest looms.
Strawberries hidden in the meadow like tiny lights.
To lie down in that fragrance now,
to reach out in the dark and pluck one —
sweetness that bursts without color —
to reach out
and not even know what it is I've taken
except that it's of the earth.

GOLDEN GATE PARK, 1969

The grey-green trees of San Francisco
fill up with fog. The park full of people;
they are listening for the last time as if
there will never again be anything
worth listening to.
The music, the last celebration, the people
walking away to the sound of their own music
strained through the evergreens, walking side by side
with a music that floats through the still trees like ghosts,
inhaling the fog which turns them old,
walking away to the sound of their own faces fading
before others take over.
The people were holding hands without even breathing.
The fog bound us together like five hundred climbers
woven into a mountain.
And shadowed on the fog the silhouette
of the next decade, the decade
that finds nothing to say, the silence
of a people unable to follow
the path of their own outrageous footsteps
and having to turn aside.
Having walked, not giving ourselves away,
as if this is where we had meant to come.

ON THE DOCK

The blonde lights on the water billow,
they are the hair of a woman in the wind,
she has no eyes, she is merely
the face of the water against the face
of the wind, they are kissing,
they have no arms, they have nothing,
they are merely
two faces of the earth in a kiss that lasts
for one chunk of timelessness.
It takes so long to know anything, and a man
lives only the length of his species. So much
comes back to me that I find no use for.
And so if our fingertips come together and it seems
the world is touching itself in two places
it means nothing, nothing lasts.
The idea of lasting was made up
by a drop of blood, a man,
a promise to himself
that things would be different
if only he could get a hold on them.
The lights will go out; it is time
to take up our lives again; if we believe
we touched, that it was real, it will put
a smile on our faces, it will do
no more than that.
The lady on the water whose hair the lights are,
the lady with fireflies in her hair whose face
blows over the water, she has no mouth to smile, no need.
The wind comes from a place beyond everything
we know. She knows,
and has no need of faith.

SNOW

Footsteps, snow against the window.
The dog twitches in its sleep. A sound
half snarl, half whimper.
You touch its neck.
A thousand centuries and still
one simple gesture is too huge
to gather in one pair of arms.
You turn your head and the shadows
turn with it, filling with hollows.
Now the dogs outside sound
far off, crazy, barking at the snow.
They lunge at drifts and come up
shaking nothing, muzzles white with snow,
as if that were enough. And maybe it is,
maybe it is. In the morning
we will go out where the children have been
making angels in the snow and see they have
no heads, no faith, no need of reason.